This igloo book belongs to:

..............................................................

**igloobooks**

Published in 2015
by Igloo Books Ltd
Cottage Farm
Sywell
NN6 0BJ
www.igloobooks.com

HUN001 0215
2 4 6 8 10 9 7 5 3 1
ISBN 978-1-78440-073-6

Written by Marilee Joy Mayfield
Illustrated by Caroline Pedler

Printed and manufactured in China

Caroline Pedler    Marilee Joy Mayfield

# I Will Always Love You

igloobooks

I will always love you because you're my **family**.
Even though I'm very small, I know you're there for me.

My dad's steps are really huge and mine are baby small.
My dad is big and very strong. He's the best of all.

My mum is kind and gentle. She's very sweet to me.
Even when I mess up, she pretends she doesn't see.

I'm ready for surprises
when Grandpa comes to stay.
Even though he's older,
he remembers how to play!

It's just a simple game
when we're rolling on the ground!

Everything is fun for me
when my brother is around.

My big sister loves to teach me
every single day.
She shows me things both big and small.
I learn as well as play.

I look up to my auntie.

She's fearless, brave and strong.

She makes me feel so safe,

I know nothing can go wrong.

Grandma tells us stories,
the best we've ever heard.
We settle at her feet
and take in every magic word.

I always have such fun when my **cousins** come to play.
We **roll** and **tumble** down the hill...

... playing snowy games **all day!**

My family is always here
to take good care of me.
When we're snuggled up at night,
we're happy as can be.

I will always love you.
You're deep inside my heart.
I'll always stay close to you...

... *We'll never be far apart.*